W9-AMB-679

BUTTERFLY FEVER

by Lori Haskins
illustrated by Jerry Smath

The Kane Press
New York

Acknowledgements: Our thanks to Dr. Dennis Frey, Biological Sciences Department, California Polytechnic State University; David F. Marriott, Ph.D., Executive Director and Founder, The Monarch Program, San Diego, California; and Karen Oberhauser, Ph.D, University of Minnesota, for helping us make this book as accurate as possible.

Book Design/Art Direction: Edward Miller

Library of Congress Cataloging-in-Publication Data

Haskins, Lori.
Butterfly fever / by Lori Haskins ; illustrated by Jerry Smath.
p. cm. — (Science solves it!)
Summary: When fourth grader Ellie and her mother leave their home in Oregon to spend a winter in Melville, California, Ellie misses her friends, but she makes new ones in school as they study monarch butterfly migration and prepare for the town's Monarch Festival.
ISBN 1-57565-134-3 (pbk. : alk. paper)
[1. Monarch butterfly—Fiction. 2. Butterflies—Fiction. 3. Moving, Household—Fiction. 4. California—Fiction.] I. Smath, Jerry, ill. II. Title. III. Series.
PZ7.H27645Bu 2004
[E]—dc21

2003011698

10 9 8 7 6 5 4 3 2

First published in the United States of America in 2004 by Kane Press, Inc.
Printed in Hong Kong.

www.kanepress.com

"California, here we come!" Ellie sang.

Ellie and her mom lived in Oregon. But this year, they were trading houses with a family from California. They'd be soaking up sunshine all winter!

After a long drive, Ellie saw a big sign—Welcome to Melville, California. "Wow!" she said. "We're here!"

She kept reading signs as they drove through town—Butterfly Bakery, Caterpillar Café. Then she spotted the school.

"Home of the Melville Monarchs," she read. "What's a monarch?"

"A kind of butterfly," her mom said.

"Figures," said Ellie. "This town is crazy about butterflies!"

They found out why when they stopped for lunch.

"Look!" Ellie said. "This says thousands of monarchs come to Melville to spend the winter. Then they leave again in the spring."

Her mom smiled. "Just like us!"

When groups of animals move from one region to another, we say that they **migrate**. Lots of animals migrate, including birds, whales, and even zebras!

Ellie started school the next day. She sat next to a girl named Tess. "You picked a great year to come to Melville!" Tess told her. "The fourth grade always keeps track of the monarchs."

"We tell the mayor when they're coming," Mr. Barr added. "Then she can start the festival!"

Why do animals migrate? To find food and water, or, like monarchs, to find a comfy spot to spend the winter. Monarchs like places that are cool and sunny.

“First we have to find people all over the Northwest to be spotters,” Mr. Barr said. “As soon as they spot the monarchs heading south, they tell us. Then we put a pin on the map to show where the monarchs are.”

"My dad will help," said Robert. "He lives in Idaho."

"I have cousins in Washington," said Tess.

Ellie felt shy, but she raised her hand. "I'll write to my friends in Oregon."

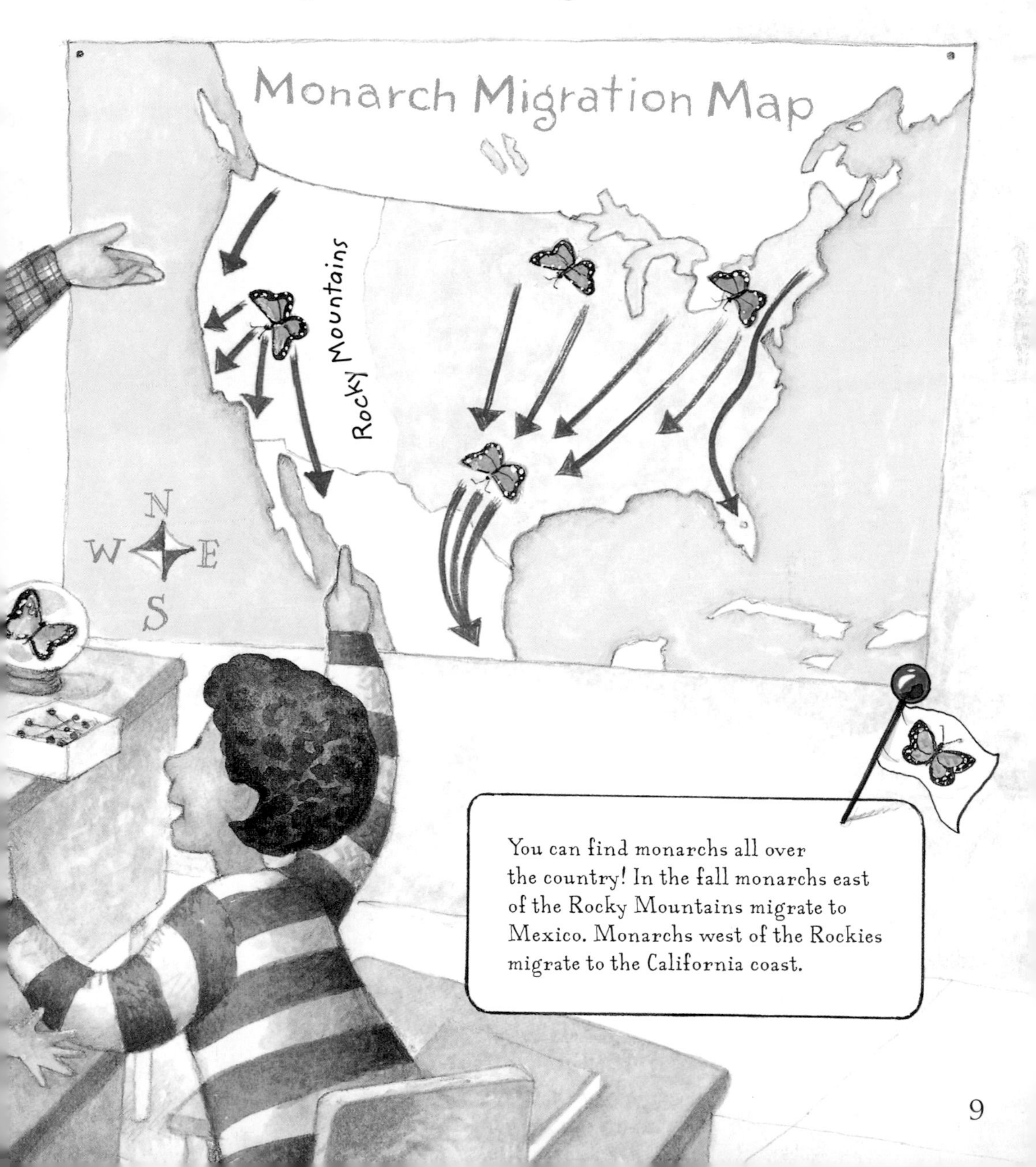

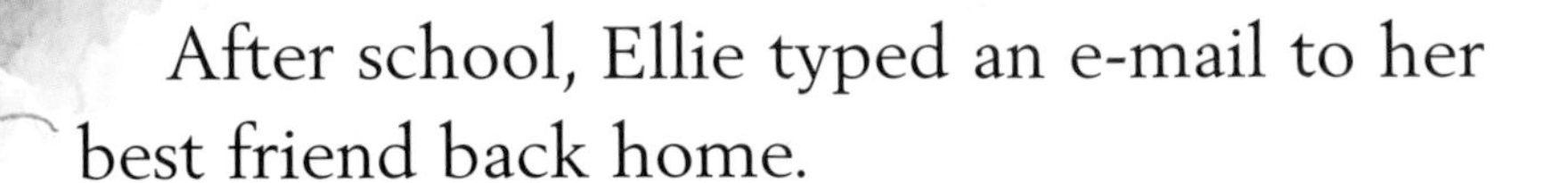

After school, Ellie typed an e-mail to her best friend back home.

Dear Lee,

I'm having fun in California. My class has a project—tracking monarch butterflies! They fly here from Oregon and lots of other places. Please write if you see any. They have bright orange-and-black wings. I'm sending you a picture so you'll know what they look like.

Love, Ellie

P.S. Say hi to Hannah and Syd! I can't wait to visit next month. I wouldn't miss your birthday party for anything!

Do monarchs migrate all at once? No. Some start their trip south in August, and some don't leave until November. The ones who get an early start usually reach their winter homes in October.

A week later, Tess heard from her cousins in Washington. The monarchs were on the move!

As the days passed, many more messages came in. One was from Lee!

Hi, Ellie,

I MISSED THEM! Every day our class looked for monarchs. Last week, everyone saw them but me. I was in bed with the flu. Now the butterflies are gone. I guess they headed south. Hope this helps.

Only TWO MORE WEEKS until vacation—and my birthday! Can't wait to see you!

Love, Lee

P.S. XOXO from Hannah and Syd

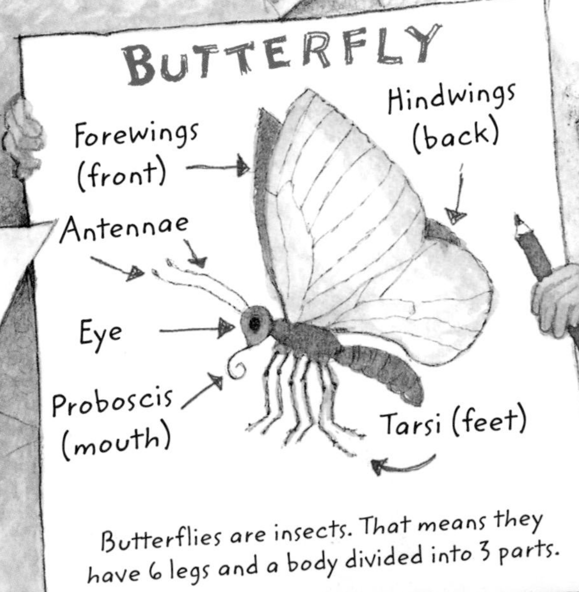

"Lee *did* help," Tess said. "I'll put a pin on the map."

"This is so cool," said Ellie. "I just wish I knew more about monarchs—as much as all of you do."

"We'll fix that," said Tess.

After school, Tess and Robert took Ellie to the nature center. "Monarchs aren't the only butterflies that migrate," said their guide, Dr. Yi. "But they fly the farthest. Some travel more than 2,000 miles!"

"Dr. Yi knows everything about monarchs!" Ellie thought.

A butterfly's wings can tell you about its life.
Perfect wings with no rips or tears mean the butterfly was born a short time ago.
A v-shaped cut means the butterfly was attacked by a bird, but got away.
Faded, raggedy wings mean a butterfly is old and doesn't have long to live.

But there was something Ellie still didn't understand. "How do the butterflies find their way?" she asked.

"Good question!" Dr. Yi said. "Some scientists think monarchs use the sun to guide them. Others think they follow rivers or mountain ranges. The truth is, no one knows for sure. It's one of nature's great mysteries!"

On the way home, Ellie started thinking about the fun things coming up—the Monarch Festival and Lee's birthday party. She couldn't wait!

Then she got a strange feeling. Suppose the monarchs came the same weekend as the party. What then?

"That just can't happen," Ellie said to herself.

But that's exactly what did happen!

"The monarchs are almost here," Ellie told her mom a few days later. "The mayor is having the festival on Saturday. Lee's party is Sunday. There's no way I can go to both."

"Oh, Ellie," her mom said. "What do you want to do?"

"I told Lee I would be there for her birthday," Ellie said. "I can't break my promise."

That week the whole town was busy getting ready for the festival. Ellie helped, but her heart felt heavy. She was leaving for Oregon on Friday. "If only I could see the festival *and* Lee," she thought.

Thursday afternoon, a van pulled into Ellie's driveway. Lee, Hannah, and Syd tumbled out!

"Oh, my gosh!" cried Ellie. "What are you guys doing here?"

"Your mom told us what was going on," said Lee. "And we thought, why not have my birthday party in California? That way we get to see you *and* the butterflies!"

"This is awesome!" said Ellie.

"This is awesome!" said Ellie again, two days later. The Monarch Festival had begun. Batons twirled. Cymbals crashed. A hundred little kids in butterfly costumes marched by.

But the best part was still to come . . .

WELCOME MONARCHS

After the parade, everyone gathered for a picnic in the park. Above, thousands of monarchs shimmered in the trees.

"It's beautiful," Ellie said with a sigh.

"They look like fall leaves," said Lee. "It's hard to believe they're real butterflies!"

"Lee! Hold still!" whispered Hannah. A butterfly had landed right on Lee's arm!

Ellie grabbed her camera and snapped a picture.

"Wow!" said Lee, as the monarch fluttered off. "What a cool birthday present!"

Monarchs gather in thick bunches in the trees. No one is sure why. It may be that they are safer from enemies in a group than on their own.

After the festival, the rest of the school year whizzed by. In March, the monarchs began to leave Melville. Ellie wrote to Lee.

Hi, Lee!

Guess what? The monarchs are leaving Melville and heading north! Along the way, they will have hundreds of baby butterflies. Those butterflies will have babies, too. The monarchs that come to Melville next fall will be the great great grandchildren of the ones that came this year. Amazing, huh?

Love, Ellie

A few months later, it was Ellie's turn to leave Melville, too.

If you want monarchs to visit you, plant milkweed. Milkweed is the only thing monarchs eat. Female monarchs always lay their eggs on milkweed leaves. Each egg is no bigger than the head of a pin!

The last day of school, the class threw Ellie a going-away party. Tess handed her a box. "This is from all of us, to remember your year in Melville."

Ellie opened up the present. Inside was a beautiful butterfly necklace. "Thank you! I love it!" said Ellie. "I'll keep it forever."

Ellie and her mom were in the car early the next morning.

"I miss home," said her mom, "but it's hard to leave Melville."

"You know what?" Ellie said. "I think we caught butterfly fever!"

THINK LIKE A SCIENTIST

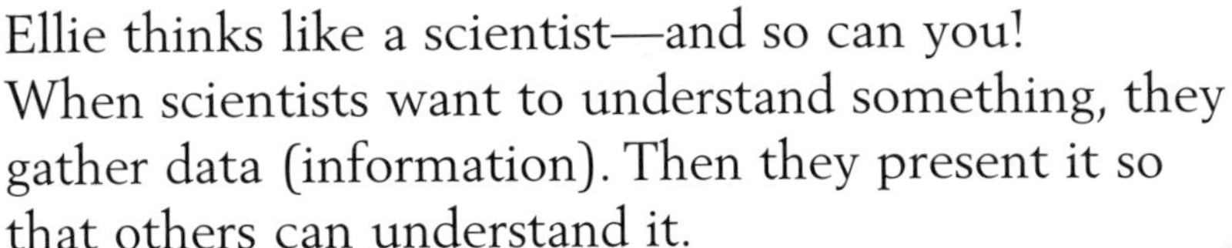

Ellie thinks like a scientist—and so can you! When scientists want to understand something, they gather data (information). Then they present it so that others can understand it.

Look Back

Maps can help us interpret or understand data. What does the map on page 9 show?

Try This!

Interpret the data in the Gray Whale Migration map to answer these questions:

- How many miles do the whales travel to get to the nursery?
- Tell about the path they take.
- A few months after the babies are born, the whales go back to their feeding grounds. How many miles do they migrate round-trip?

What other information does the map give you?

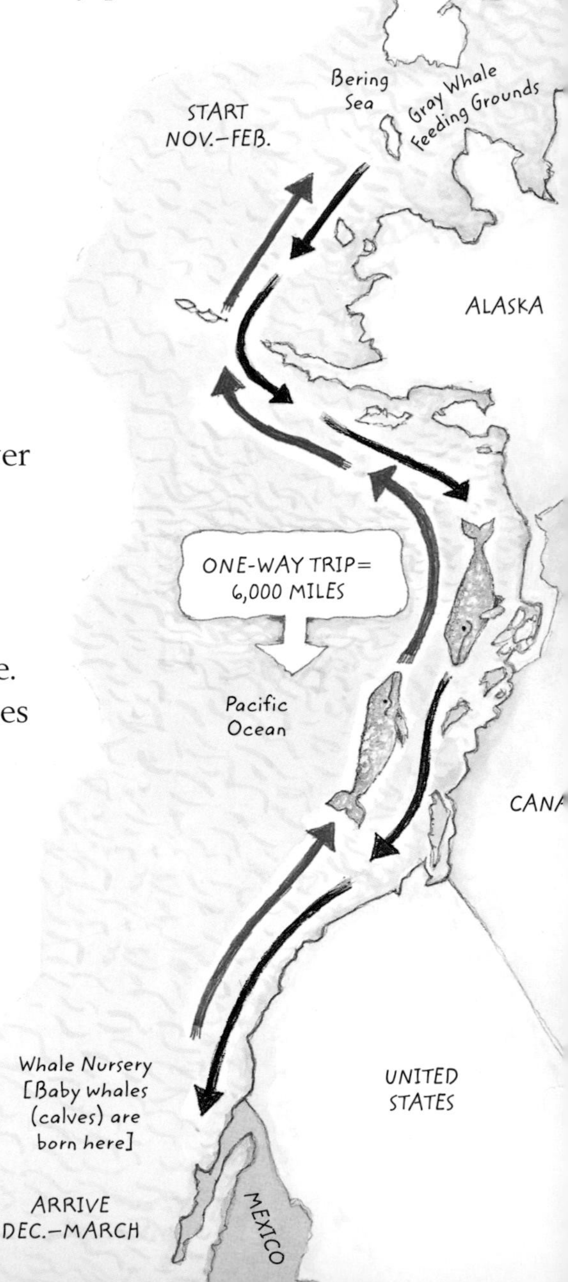